Zoe and Tomato

Written by Catherine Baker
Illustrated by Javier Joaquín

Collins

Who's in this story?

Listen and say 

 Download the audio at www.collins.co.uk/839825

HOSPITAL

Grandma

Zoe, Mum and Dad lived in a small house with a blue door. They all liked playing in the garden and going for bike rides.

Zoe loved her Mum and Dad, and
Mum and Dad loved Zoe, too.

One day, Mum and Dad said, “Come here, Zoe! We want to talk to you.”

Zoe sat down between Mum and Dad. “What is it?” she asked.

“A new baby is coming!” said Mum. “The baby is your sister.” Mum was very happy.

“Oh,” said Zoe.

She was sad. “I don’t want a sister,” thought Zoe.

Dad hugged Zoe. “Don’t worry!” he said. “Sisters are fantastic!”

But Zoe looked at the floor and said, “I don’t want a sister.”

“I know!” said Mum. “You can choose a name for the new baby, Zoe!”

“Can I choose any name?” said Zoe.

“Yes,” said Mum. “Any name you like.”

All day Zoe thought about names for the baby. “I don’t like babies!” She thought. “What other things don’t I like?”

“Tomatoes,” thought Zoe. “I don’t like tomatoes. I know! Baby Tomato is a good name!”

Zoe smiled. She liked the new baby’s name.

After many weeks, Mum's tummy was bigger.

One day, Grandma came to Zoe's house. She played lots of games with Zoe. Grandma and Zoe always had fun.

Then Mum and Dad went to the hospital.
Zoe was safe at home with Grandma.

In the morning, Dad phoned Grandma.

"We have a new baby!" he said.

"How exciting, Zoe!" said Grandma.

But Zoe was sad. She thought it was not exciting.

“Let’s go to the hospital,” said Grandma.

At the hospital, Mum showed Zoe the new baby.

“Here is your sister, Zoe!” she said. “You can hold her!”

Zoe looked at the baby. The baby was very small and red.

"Tomato is a good name for her," thought Zoe.

Zoe held the small, red baby. She smiled. “I like you,” thought Zoe. “I don’t want to call you Tomato.”

Zoe hugged the small baby.

"Did you choose a name for the baby, Zoe?" asked Dad.

Zoe smiled. “Yes,” she said. “Can we call her Poppy?”

“That’s a beautiful name, Zoe!” said Mum. “Why Poppy?”

“That’s easy,” said Zoe. “A poppy is a pretty, red flower and my sister is a pretty, red baby!”

Picture dictionary

Listen and repeat 

hospital

hug

poppy

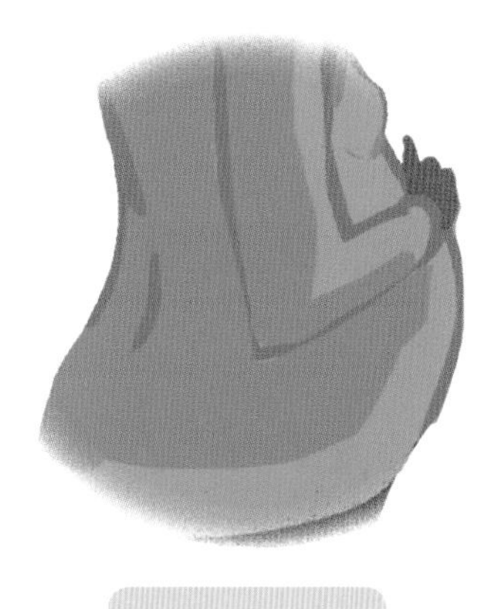

tummy

1 Look and order the story

2 Listen and say  

Collins

Published by Collins
An imprint of HarperCollins*Publishers*
Westerhill Road
Bishopbriggs
Glasgow
G64 2QT

HarperCollins*Publishers*
1st Floor, Watermarque Building
Ringsend Road
Dublin 4
Ireland

William Collins' dream of knowledge for all began with the publication of his first book in 1819.

A self-educated mill worker, he not only enriched millions of lives, but also founded a flourishing publishing house. Today, staying true to this spirit, Collins books are packed with inspiration, innovation and practical expertise. They place you at the centre of a world of possibility and give you exactly what you need to explore it.

10 9 8 7 6 5 4 3 2

ISBN 978-0-00-839825-5

www.collins.co.uk/elt

British Library Cataloguing in Publication Data

A catalogue record for this publication is available from the British Library.

Author: Catherine Baker
Illustrator: Javier Joaquín (Beehive)
Series editor: Rebecca Adlard
Commissioning editor: Fiona Undrill
Publishing manager: Lisa Todd
Product managers: Jennifer Hall and Caroline Green
In-house editor: Alma Puts Keren
Project manager: Emily Hooton
Editor: Matthew Hancock
Proofreaders: Natalie Murray and Michael Lamb
Cover designer: Kevin Robbins
Typesetter: 2Hoots Publishing Services Ltd
Audio produced by id audio, London
Reading guide author: Emma Wilkinson
Production controller: Rachel Weaver
Printed and bound by: GPS Group, Slovenia

MIX
Paper from responsible sources
FSC™ C007454

This book is produced from independently certified FSC™ paper to ensure responsible forest management.

For more information visit: **www.harpercollins.co.uk/green**

Download the audio for this book and a reading guide for parents and teachers at www.collins.co.uk/839825